GUNFIRE AT GETTYSBURG

BY R.A. MONTGOMERY

ILLUSTRATED BY TOM LA PADULA

An R.A. Montgomery Book

A BANTAM SKYLARK BOOK®
NEW YORK · TORONTO · LONDON · SYDNEY · AUCKLAND

RL4, age 10 and up

GUNFIRE AT GETTYSBURG

A Bantam Book/September 1994

CHOOSE YOUR OWN ADVENTURE® is a registered
trademark of Bantam Books, a division of Bantam Doubleday
Dell Publishing Group, Inc. Registered in U.S. Patent and
Trademark Office and elsewhere.

Original conception of Edward Packard
Cover art by David Mattingly
Interior illustrations by Tom La Padula

ISBN 0-553-56393-9

Published simultaneously in the United States and Canada

Bantam Books are published by Bantam Books, a division of
Bantam Doubleday Dell Publishing Group, Inc. Its trademark,
consisting of the words "Bantam Books" and the portrayal of a
rooster, is Registered in U.S. Patent and Trademark Office and
in other countries. Marca Registrada. Bantam Books, 1540
Broadway, New York, New York 10036.

PRINTED IN THE UNITED STATES OF AMERICA

OPM   0 9 8 7 6 5 4 3 2 1

GUNFIRE AT GETTYSBURG

WARNING!!!

Do not read this book straight through from beginning to end. These pages contain many different adventures that you may have with the Confederate and Federal armies in the historic Battle of Gettysburg. From time to time as you read along, you will be asked to make a choice. Your choice may lead to success or disaster!

The adventures you have are the results of your choices. You are responsible because you choose. After you make your decision, follow the instructions to find out what happens to you next.

Think carefully before you act. You may have the chance to meet General Robert E. Lee and assist him in a decisive victory. But do you really want to endanger yourself and possibly your family by going behind enemy lines? And what will your country be like when the war is over?

Good luck!

AUTHOR'S NOTE

During three hot days in July of 1863, the greatest and bloodiest battle ever fought on American soil blasted its way across the hills and fields around a little town in Pennsylvania.

The Battle of Gettysburg was the turning point of the American Civil War. In three previous years of fighting, the Confederate forces of the South had defeated their Union opponents in almost every battle. All these Confederate victories occurred on Southern ground, most in Virginia. But in late June of 1863 the main Confederate army, under General Robert E. Lee, secretly invaded the North, crossing into the lush farm country of southern Pennsylvania.

Just a few miles into Pennsylvania lay the little town of Gettysburg. Roads from different directions came together here, and—almost by accident—so did the two armies. As General Lee's army marched north, his cavalry rode out to learn where the Union army was. But the Union army, also called the Federals, learned that Lee was moving, and they too began marching from the blasted fields of Virginia up into Pennsylvania. The Federals didn't realize it, but their movement cut Lee off from his cavalry. So before the armies collided, the Confederates couldn't learn much about the landscape around them—and they didn't know where their enemy was.

As usual, the Confederates were heavily outnumbered. There were seventy-three thousand men in Lee's Army of Northern Virginia, while the bluecoated Army of the Potomac had some ninety-five thousand soldiers. No one expected all those men to fight in this town, but when they did, the whole war was at stake. If the Southerners had won, the North would have lain wide open for them to conquer.

Before you begin your adventure, you should know a few things about how the Civil War was fought. Most soldiers on both sides carried muskets, heavy firearms that had to be loaded one shot at a time. The Civil War musket was actually an early type of rifle: the inside of its barrel was grooved, or "rifled," to spin the bullet and fire it farther and more accurately. Officers often carried pistols and swords.

Artillery batteries, which played a big part at Gettysburg, fired heavy cannons. These were loaded with solid iron balls or shells, hollow balls filled with gunpowder, and sometimes also with small metal balls. When they hit, all the weapons of Gettysburg—especially the cannon shells—did terrible damage.

I hope this story gives you a strong experience of just how important this battle was—and just how terrible, too. If you'd like to learn more, there are many great books about Gettysburg and the Civil War. (You may also be able to visit Gettysburg National Military Park, where the real battlefield is carefully preserved and explained.) We must never forget what really happened at the little town of Gettysburg on those hot days in 1863. Once you've had your own adventure there, I hope you'll understand why.

Doug Wilhelm

It's Tuesday, but there's no school—it's summertime. Tomorrow is the first day of July, 1863. There's a war on, the great and terrible War of Secession. But for three years it has raged far away from your peaceful town in southern Pennsylvania.

Far away, that is, until now.

This afternoon, gray clouds hang heavily over the long ripples of green woods and golden fields that frame your town. The fields are ripe, but no one is cutting the wheat. People say soldiers are marching this way. The whole town seems frozen in suspense.

All except for you and your best friend.

"I'll be the Rebs this time," says Billy Bayley, a sandy-haired farmer's son.

"No, you won't," you answer. You crouch low and aim your long stick. "You're the Yanks and you'll charge. Then I'll mow you down."

"But you always get to be the Rebs," Billy says. "And you always mow me down."

"Well, that's what always happens," you snap. "Don't I read the papers? The Yanks always blunder into some trap, and the Rebs mow 'em down. Now play your part, Billy Bayley."

"I won't. Not this time," he snaps back.

"No need to play at battles," calls a man from the road nearby. "You'll see one shortly."

"Oh, surely," you answer sarcastically. "People have said that for weeks and nothing's happened. Nobody's going to fight over a little town like Gettysburg."

Turn to page 42.

You're being offered a once-in-a-lifetime chance to meet the legendary Robert E. Lee—and maybe to play a role in history. But right now Lee's army is overrunning your hometown.

Maybe you *should* run after them—see if your family is all right. But even if they're in danger, what could you do? And even if this officer doesn't shoot, what about the Rebel troops?

The officer nods toward Seminary Ridge. His hand rests on the hilt of his sword.

"I'd suggest you come along," he says.

You've got to choose—now.

If you agree to meet General Lee, turn to page 25.

If you make a run for Gettysburg, turn to page 10.

The school sits atop one long ripple called Seminary Ridge, just outside the town. In a few minutes you've sneaked into the main building and tiptoed up to the cupola.

"Oh, my gosh," says Billy Bayley.

Along the west rises South Mountain, a long, forested bank eight miles away. All its cleared spots are crawling with tiny figures. Dozens on dozens of little smoke trails rise from the mountainside.

You realize the rumors are true: General Lee's troops *have* invaded the North. You're looking at the campfires of the Army of Northern Virginia.

From behind you, back in town, you hear cheering and the pounding of hooves. Among the houses you glimpse horsemen clad in blue.

"The Union cavalry," you whisper. "We might see a skirmish after all."

Turn to page 54.

4

As evening settles in, campfires flare up all over the fields behind Seminary Ridge. The Rebel officer leads you to a group of large tents.

From the guards posted all around, you know this is the command post—the new field headquarters of the Army of Northern Virginia. The officer nods to a sentry, then speaks to some men in gray outside one of the tents. They look at you, their foreheads wrinkling. Finally one of the men shrugs, nods, and opens the tent flap.

Your officer turns and motions for you to follow.

You step into the tent. A lamp casts yellow light inside. A gray-haired man, bending over a table, starts to rise. Your breath stops. You're staring at Robert E. Lee, general of the Confederate States of America.

You've never seen a more dignified-looking man. Gray-bearded and handsome, General Lee seems commanding but also gentle. Your officer speaks softly to him. General Lee turns to you and nods. His eyes are deep and sad.

"Hello, my young friend," he says. "I understand you're an expert on this terrain."

"Well," you say, "I guess I know the area."

"That's good," General Lee says. "Because this fight has just begun—and I don't like the situation my army is in."

You don't know what he means. The Rebels have won the upper hand—you saw it yourself. What does Lee know that you don't?

Turn to page 107.

But out there is just where you want to be. You've seen a lot of soldiers around, but you need to climb atop the ridge to get a full look at the Union defenses. How can you do that now?

The house's little kitchen is steamy and hot. The stocky cook dumps your sack of bread on the counter. "Excellent," he says. "Just right for General Meade's luncheon meeting with the field commanders. Now get to work slicing these." He hands you a knife and walks out of the kitchen.

The door's at your back. You could slip out now—hurry to the ridge crest, take a look, and then try to get out of here. Or you could stay. If this General Meade is the top commander, you might be able to overhear the Union battle plan.

If you slip out, turn to page 82.

If you stay, turn to page 74.

You scramble down the branches and leap to the ground after Billy. You start sprinting back toward Gettysburg—but you both stop short.

Coming at you on a dead run is the whole Union army!

Thousands of bluecoats are chugging into the fight, their ammunition cases flapping, their faces red and streaked with sweat. They fill the land between you and safety. Some are already firing—right your way.

"What now?" yells Billy.

Your only hope is to veer right—to try and squirt out sideways before these two armies collide right here.

"Run to the ridge. To the seminary," you yell. "Go!"

Turn to page 68.

Under the moonlight, all of Seminary Ridge and the fields behind it have become one long field hospital. The wounded lie against every tree, all over the grass and the trampled-down fields. In the open air, surgeons hack off arms and legs, leaving them in piles.

In the days and weeks to come every farmhouse outside town and almost every building in town is crammed with wounded men.

You labor for days and nights and days. You bring water, cut bread, make coffee and tea for the men. You make many, many friends. One day, two of these new friends—a bearded New Yorker named John Tinker and a baby-faced Georgian, Steve Dooley—stop you in your rounds. Tinker's lost an arm, Dooley a leg.

"We've got something for you," says Tinker.

"Stoop here, by my bed," says Dooley.

Puzzled, you bend toward him. Dooley takes out a shiny piece of red ribbon. Hanging from its end are two flattened minié balls.

"They took these out of us," says Tinker. "One from Dooley, the other from me. We've made them into a medal for you."

Dooley loops the ribbon over your neck. All around you, men are watching. Now they applaud.

Shyly, you smile. "I'll never forget this," you say.

"Neither will we," say the Rebel and the Yankee.

The End

"I've got to go," you tell the Confederate. "My family's in that town."

He nods. "I understand."

You turn and start to run. But then you stop and turn back.

"Some say all the Rebels are devils—murderers," you tell the slender blond officer. "Others say they're heroes, or gentlemen, or the toughest soldiers ever. Which is so?"

He considers a moment. "I've been in this war three years," he says. "I've seen every type you mention—on both sides. Neither side's the devil. And neither one's all angels."

"Then what's this war about?"

"States' rights versus Union," he says quickly, as if he's said it a thousand times.

"What does that mean?"

"Up north you've got factories, and whole cities full of machines and men to keep you strong and rich. We've got cotton and slaves, and not a lot else. We need our slaves for our cotton, or we're ruined. Your president, your Union would outlaw slavery. Our states say our slaves are our right."

"So that's what it's about? Slaves?"

He nods. "Slaves or ruination."

"But aren't slaves people?"

He ignores your question.

"What's your name?" he asks.

You tell him.

Go on to the next page.

"I'm Cole," he says. "Colonel Jason Cole, Forty-eighth Georgia Infantry."

"Do you believe in your cause, Colonel?"

"I do," he says firmly. "We're fighting for our homeland—our way of life. You Yankees would trample it. Now go. See to your family."

He turns away. You start to run toward town.

Turn to page 28.

At this moment, in this place, the tide of Gettysburg starts to turn. In years to come you'll read and talk many times about this small but vital charge: how the Twentieth Maine Regiment, fighting at the end of the Union line on Little Round Top against the battle-tough Fifteenth Alabama, ran almost completely out of ammunition. Knowing the battle—even the war —was at stake, the Maine commander ordered his men to fix their bayonets and charge.

You watch the shouting Maine soldiers rush at the Rebels. For a second the Confederate fighters stop, as if they can't believe what's happening. Then the Fifteenth Alabama—which has never before been defeated in battle—turns and clatters back down the hill.

Next thing you know there's a stampede of retreating Confederates and a storm of Union guns firing right at you. There's wild confusion— men are dropping everything to get away from this deadly fire. You crouch behind a rock.

The ground is covered with the dead, mangled, and badly wounded. There are so many, you could never bring them all to safety. The air above your head whistles with musket fire. You want to get away, if you can make it. But all around you men cry and plead for help.

Should you join the wild retreat, or stay with your stretcher and keep bringing wounded soldiers to safety?

If you fall back, turn to page 81.

If you stay, turn to page 70.

14

It's late. You're lying very still, wrapped in an itchy Rebel blanket.

Your guard leans against a tree. He's finally snoring. The camp is dark and quiet. A lamp still burns in Lee's tent.

Your mind has been churning with the tales you've heard of how the Rebels treat their prisoners. The stories are awful—of Southern prison camps where the captives are crammed together like worms in a can, with filth and disease everywhere and no shelter from the broiling sun. It is said that it's better to die on the battlefield than be taken prisoner by the Rebs.

Is all this true—or just a lot of horror stories?

Now's your chance. If you can just sneak out of Lee's camp, no one will know you're a prisoner with life-and-death information. They'll just see a local kid. Billy Bayley's house is not far off beyond Seminary Ridge. If you can make it there, you'll be free. No one need know what you told Robert E. Lee.

But the Rebels have been decent to you—gentlemanly. Maybe once the battle is over they'll let you go. Maybe you shouldn't take a chance on escaping now.

It's time to decide.

*If you stay in Lee's camp,
turn to page 77.*

*If you try to sneak away,
turn to page 41.*

In the woods all around, in the fields ahead of you, shells thud and explode. Nobody's guarding you. Lee sits alone on his stump. Nobody speaks to him or brings him messages. It's as if he has given his orders and the battle is now out of his hands.

You think fast. Billy Bayley's farmhouse is behind Seminary Ridge, back of the Rebel lines and behind the targets of the Union gunners. You'd better make a dash for it.

You look back one last time. But Lee is looking away, gazing at the smoke. You dash over to the dirt road that leads along the ridge.

All at once you're caught in a crowd of young men. Some look like boys. They're all running down the ridge, carrying long, narrow objects.

"Come on!" yells a man with stripes on his arm. He grabs your collar and yanks you forward.

"But—"

"Forget the buts!" the man yells. "In an hour there'll be men down everywhere. Now move!"

"No, I . . ."

The man stops. He sticks his face in yours.

"I'm Avery Hill—*Sergeant* Avery Hill. This is the Drum Corps, Second South Carolina Infantry. We're a stretcher crew now. This whole war's coming to a head this afternoon—every free hand's got to help bring out wounded. I don't see you carrying any musket, so now you're a stretcher-bearer, too."

You gulp. "Okay," you say.

Turn to page 113.

"Here's the town," you say, drawing a rectangle. You sketch Seminary Ridge. "We're here. Just past the other side of town are those two hills, right close together—Cemetery Hill and Culp's Hill."

"The Federals are concentrating on those hills now," says Lee.

"Cemetery Ridge runs down from the graveyard. It's mostly open ground, with some stone walls and such," you say, sketching it. "That's right across from where we are now."

"Which is higher?" asks Lee. "Our ridge or theirs?"

You look seriously at Lee. "Theirs is higher."

"I was afraid of that," Lee muses.

"General, why not attack now?" Colonel Cole says. "The Federals are reeling. We could finish them tonight."

Slowly Lee nods. "I've given orders that General Ewell's men are to do that—*if* they are able. But this day's fighting has been dreadful. Our men are exhausted. It appears General Ewell has decided not to push them farther.

"But tonight we have many more troops coming up," Lee continues. "The enemy is here"— he points to the hills and ridge beyond town— "and tomorrow I shall strike him." He turns to you. "The question is, where?"

In fact, you know just where the Rebels should strike. But should you tell Lee—and perhaps give the battle, and even the war, to the Confederacy?

Turn to page 71.

18

"No more gawkin'," McPherson says. "We got to move."

"Well, uh, I really should go."

"Sorry, Rabbit! You missed your chance. Now we go to work."

The wagon draws up to an artillery battery, three guns on the ridge crest near a clump of trees. The crews hurry toward you as McPherson climbs into the back of the wagon. He jerks his thumb for you to follow.

"We lift 'em one at a time and pass 'em to the boys," McPherson says, nodding at the artillerymen. "Now lift these shells *careful*. They're heavy and they don't want to be dropped."

The first shell is so heavy your arms strain away from your shoulders—but grunting, you help lift it. Sweat runs stinging into your eyes. It's blisteringly hot. One after another you and McPherson unload the shells—but the work seems to take ages. You've got to get away, somehow. But how? If you just run, what'll happen?

You decide you've got to take the chance. You're set to leap from the wagon and hightail it, just as the big redhead said, when you hear a clap of thunder from the Rebel side.

You stop and look up. The sky is clear.

Then the world explodes.

Turn to page 49.

You move among the wounded, stooping to offer words of kindness. "The battle's over now," you whisper. "You're safe. Help is coming." Soon Hill returns with a water jug, a tin cup, and an armload of blankets.

"Here, take the water," he says.

You carry the jug from man to man. With cracked lips they drink. Some nod, a few smile thinly. One man whispers, "You're a lifesaver."

You like the sound of that. You're glad you decided to stick with this.

And stick with it you do. You've got no idea how many casualties the Battle of Gettysburg will produce—about forty-three thousand in all, almost one-third of all the soldiers brought here by the two armies. The fight will climax the next day with a great Rebel charge against the middle of Cemetery Ridge. The attack, later called Pickett's Charge after one of the commanders who leads it, will fail. Thousands more men will be left for you stretcher-bearers to pick up.

And it will be days before a single ambulance wagon reaches the bloodstained rocks around Little Round Top—scene of some of the worst slaughter in the Civil War. Despite your best efforts to help them, dozens of the men that you've rescued from the battle will never leave this forest alive.

But right now you just continue your work, trying to help the wounded among the rocks and trees. Finally, at night, you stagger through the woods and up the ridge.

Turn to page 9.

Even Avery Hill stops to watch.

Halfway down the rocky open slopes of the low hill, a line of bluecoats is battling so close to the Rebel attackers that their muskets almost touch. Smoke gusts up, and darts of flame stab through it as the bluecoated fighters rise from behind stone walls to blast straight into the Confederates.

The Federals must have rushed troops over the back of Little Round Top just in time to meet the Rebel assault. To the left along the spreading valley rises the smoke and crashing of a terrible battle. This is the edge of everything. If the Rebels can break the Union line and take this hill, they'll have the whole Yankee army below them in their sights.

And this duel on the hill has got to break soon. The Yankees are holding on, but the Rebels are pushing more men up the hill. They're hammering and blasting at the blue line. You're sure the bluecoats are about to give way when something wild and surprising happens.

There's a roar of men's voices—but it's not the Rebel Yell. Over the right shoulder of the hill comes a charge of bluecoats. Sunlight glints off their bayonets, and they don't stop to fire. Instead they swing like a gate that closes smack into the side of the Confederates.

Turn to page 12.

There's a long silence. Finally, gravely, your father speaks.

"You must go," he says.

"Thanks!" You dash up the steps.

"Please be careful," your mother calls. "Don't get killed!" But you're moving too fast to answer.

The black-eyed soldier stops you in the kitchen. "I told you to go down to the cellar," he says.

"But . . . I have to go out."

"No, you don't. It's too dangerous. Go downstairs."

"But . . ."

"Go!" This time he points the pistol at you.

You go back down.

"I've got to get out," you tell your family. "I know—the coal chute!"

Turn to page 45.

The big redhead whips the horses hard, and they wheel the wagon back downhill. Shells crash and explode all around. Dirt and stones shower you as you jolt down the slope.

"What now?" you shout through the mayhem.

"I've got to bring up more shells," he yells. "But you're getting out of this! Soon as we get off the ridge, I'm sending you . . ."

A very close whistling drowns him out. McPherson lunges to cover your body with his.

The explosion seems to happen in slow motion. You're in the air, hurtling through it, falling and falling until you thud onto the ground in a heap. Your face scrapes the dirt.

Now you're on hands and knees, shaking your head to clear it. Blood drips down, but your fingers find only a scrape on your forehead.

You glance around. McPherson looks bad.

The big man lies twenty feet away; you can see blood pumping from his leg. You rush to him and kneel, staring at the wet gash.

"Go, Rabbit," he gasps. "Git away. Please!"

And you want to get away—if you can. You're terrified and panicky—you want to run and run until all this noise and horror is far behind you.

But if you leave now, McPherson will die. If you stay and press hard on his wound, you may be able to stop the bleeding and save his life.

If you stay to help McPherson, turn to page 86.

If you try to make it to safety, turn to page 94.

24

"All right," you say to Lee. "I'll try it."

The general nods. "Good. Stay here tonight. I won't place you under guard again. I know you can be trusted." He turns back to gaze at tomorrow's battlefield.

You spend the evening wandering the Confederate encampments along Seminary Ridge. Under the soft, bright glow of a full moon, the Rebel soldiers sit quietly around their campfires. In the distance is the sound of hard fighting. Gone are the high spirits of the night before.

"We fought them as hard as we ever have," you hear one soldier say. "And we hardly gained an inch."

"They've got the high ground," says another Rebel.

"It's their *own* ground, too," says a third. "We ain't in Virginia anymore."

"I think the Yanks are finally turning into soldiers," says the first.

"We've got a fight on our hands, that's sure," another soldier says. "But we'll git 'em tomorrow."

You walk on. Crowds of wounded men line the road. The night air is thick with their moans and painful cries. A scream rips through. You hurry on—but as far up the road as you can see, the wounded go on and on. You hear the men moving, sighing, weeping, whispering the names of people they love. You'll never forget the sights and sounds of this night of July 2, 1863.

Turn to page 98.

There's probably nothing you can do in town. You decide to meet the commander of the Confederates.

"I'll go with you," you tell the officer.

He leads you down Seminary Ridge. On this early evening, everything is different. The dirt roads you've explored so often are crowded with Rebel soldiers. So are the woods and fields. Skinny, dirty men are moving in everywhere.

These soldiers aren't flashy. Many don't even wear uniforms—just the ragged shirts of poor farmers. Those who are in uniform wear simple gray or butternut-colored jackets, with a rolled blanket slung around their chests and a musket in their grip. Many are barefoot; others have tied filthy rags around their feet. Only some wear dusty boots.

But the Rebels have fiery eyes. They shout and clap each other on the back as they draw into campsites. You see tents going up. Men who've marched and fought their way up from Virginia haul scraps of wood and pieces of farm fencing. Everyone around you is flushed with the day's victory.

"Is the battle over?" you ask the fair-haired officer.

"Oh, no—the Yanks don't quit that easily," he answers. "But I'll tell you this: The Federal army that's falling back through your town right now is all that stands between us and Washington, D.C. Once we win this battle, we'll have won the war."

Turn to page 4.

You give Rena a nod—and you both run.

But the tall grass slows you down. The Rebel soldiers shout, "Hey! Stop!"

Cemetery Ridge is a long distance ahead.

"Keep going!" you mutter. As she runs, Rena looks back at the soldiers.

Ahead of her a dark figure rises. "Rena," you yell. "Look out!" But she's still looking back and doesn't see this Rebel picket swing his musket, butt end first. It slams into her head, knocks off her hat, and she goes down.

You gaze down at your friend. She's stirring slowly.

The picket aims his musket at you. "Walk back toward our lines," he says.

"No. I'm staying with her."

"No, you ain't. You stay here and I'll shoot you. You walk and I'll let you go. Either way, she's going back where she belongs."

"She was *born* here!"

"Don't make no difference. A slave's a slave."

"Why, you—" You shove the gun barrel up, startling the soldier. But by now the other pickets have caught up. One of them grabs you.

"Go," he says. "There's nothing you can do."

You take a last look at Lorena. You hope she can escape, somehow, before they ship her South. Or that the war ends. Or something.

Slowly you turn, and without a word you walk back through the moonlit grass. You know, somehow, that you'll never find out what happens to Lorena. And you never do.

The End

Fences are trampled and brown craters have been gouged all across the open fields that lead into Gettysburg. Bodies lie everywhere.

The noise in town is raucous and surging, like a huge crowd at the county fair. There are shouts and cheers, and sometimes shots—popping and cracking sounds. You follow the railroad tracks into town to the little station on Baltimore Street.

Gettysburg's main street is a surging, rowdy crowd of strangers—stringy, ragged men in gray, butternut, and motley clothes. They grip muskets and fill the narrow avenue.

This is a mob. Some men fire their muskets into the air. You watch in horror as several pound on the door of a home, then crack it open with their rifle butts. They rush inside, shouting.

Are they killing people? Robbing houses? You duck back along the tracks, sprinting for the back way home. You're hoping you can beat the Rebels there.

Turn to page 78.

A crowd of running feet outside the window throws long shadows on the wall. You all crouch down, and you shudder. You know they're Rebel soldiers.

"You've got to help her," says Anna.

"Me? How?"

"I don't know—but no one knows this town like you do. You've got to get her to the Union side. She's our friend."

"But . . . what about my family? I was going to see about them."

Rena Solver's dark eyes catch yours. "You do what you have to," she says. "I can take care of myself."

You're not sure about that. Someone's got to help her—and you're the only one who can. Yet shouldn't you first at least find out if your family's alive?

If you try to help Lorena Solver escape, turn to page 64.

If you go see about your family first, turn to page 110.

"Relax," says Billy Bayley. "This is Joe Tibbets. Joe's from North Carolina."

"That's right—Twenty-sixth North Carolina Infantry," says the Rebel softly. He's very young.

"Last night," Billy says, "around midnight, Mother and I were trying to sleep. We heard a knock on the door. It turned out to be Joe."

"Yesterday was my first battle," the young soldier tells you. "I went through it all right—I didn't run. But up on that hill there, my regiment was running to the fight when some Yanks rose up from behind a stone wall right alongside us. We'd never seen 'em. In less time than it takes to say this, every Yankee fired and every single man in my regiment but me was down. All of them dead, or hurt so bad it was awful to see. I . . . I'm only fifteen years old."

"Fifteen!"

"Yes. I wanted to see the war. But now I've seen it, and I never want to see it no more."

"We told Joe he could stay with us," says Billy. "We'll give him some of my clothes. He's about my size. You better stay here, too," he adds, "till the battle's over."

"I will," you say. "I've seen enough, too. I don't think it matters who wins, Billy Bayley. This is no game."

In fact, Joe Tibbets stays in Gettysburg for the rest of his life. You and Billy often relate your adventures in the great battle, but you keep Joe's identity secret—because you were there, and you know how it was.

The End

Rena's probably right about the man helping the wounded. "Let's just see what he wants," you say. "Keep your cap pulled low."

An older man with a sandy mustache strides up. "We could use a hand with these wounded," he says. "We're surgeons—C.S.A." You know that stands for Confederate States of America. "If you could just bring water to these men for a little while," he tells you, "it'd be a big help."

"Well, okay," you say. "For just a bit—then we got to get back."

"Fine. Come to the wagon with me." At the ambulance wagon the surgeon hands you a jug. He holds out a tin cup for Lorena. She reaches for it, but you quickly shove her hand away.

"I'll get that," you say. The surgeon is looking at your hand. Did he notice hers? You can't tell.

"Who do we give water to?" you ask.

"Whoever's alive," says the doctor.

"Just Confederates?"

"Oh, no. Whoever's alive."

For the next half hour or so you and Lorena move among the blood-soaked victims of the battle. Whenever someone looks up or calls to you, you pour a cup and Lorena bends to give him a drink.

"Bless you, sister," a soldier says to her.

You grow so absorbed in helping these men that you don't think about the danger. When a detachment of Rebel soldiers emerges from town, you don't notice the Confederate surgeon speaking to them and pointing your way.

Turn to page 61.

You catch Lorena's eyes and nod—very quickly and slightly—toward the Union side. Now you turn, choose the closest Rebel picket, and lunge at him.

He's shocked—you've gained a split second of surprise. You knock his rifle barrel up. The other two soldiers converge on you. You wheel to see a musket butt raised at you, but you dodge the blow. You duck under the soldier and light out, away from the direction in which Lorena has escaped.

"I'll shoot!" a picket shouts behind you.

There's a blast from behind—now another. You dive into the tall grass. Bullets whiz above your head. You lie as flat as you possibly can, shoving your face into the dirt.

Now there's a fusillade of shots—but these come from up ahead. You don't know what's happening. From the Rebel pickets comes more firing, but it doesn't seem aimed at you. What's going on?

Cautiously you poke up your head. The Rebels are firing toward Cemetery Ridge. From that direction you see stabs of flame firing back at them. The shots at you triggered a volley from the Union pickets!

For the moment in the sudden fight you're forgotten. You can't see Lorena. You'd best try to make it to the Union lines—if you can. And you'd better get there before this spasm of gunfire ends and the Rebels come looking for you.

Turn to page 109.

Across the wall that the Union soldiers had been set to defend rages a wild struggle, a musket-firing and bayonet-stabbing crowd of blue and gray men all mixed together. They fill the few yards in front of the wall. Everywhere beyond, the long, flattened field is dense with fallen gray men.

You must have been out for a while.

You stare across the fields at the many men struggling to drag themselves back to Lee's line. The dead and wounded are strewn in tangled crowds. Here by the wall, the one gray mass that made it this far is furiously attacking the Union defenders. They're charging, swinging swords and jabbing bayonets, climbing over the wall into the teeth of Union fire that flashes and blows men backward. But the holes fill and more men in gray push to break the line, just as Lee said they would.

Always afterward this great attack by fifteen thousand Confederates, the divisions of Generals Pettigrew and Pickett, will be famous as Pickett's Charge. Its final, terrible climax is raging in front of you.

Here the stone wall angles away from you, then cuts over in front of a clump of trees. At those trees the Rebels have made it over the wall. They're cutting fiercely at the Federals who are turning to flee by the dozens.

The Federals are giving way! Is this the moment the South wins the war? And why is there no noise?

Turn to page 59.

36

You wait in the woods with the drummers for an hour or more. It's late afternoon. Beyond the woods ahead the noise builds and builds. At first it's a widespread crackling, like dozens of firecrackers. Then it grows into a storm, a raging of terrible roars as muskets fire over and over. Yells and screams drift through the trees.

You wish you knew how the battle was going. Why is there so much firing? Did the Federals get troops onto Little Round Top before the Rebels attacked?

Avery Hill moves among your group, shouting over the noise. Men stand and lift their stretchers.

"You'll work with me," Hill yells at you. He grabs one end of your stretcher and unrolls the canvas slung between the two poles.

He nods ahead and starts running through the woods. You keep up, stumbling now and then.

You know this area. Beyond the woods there's a rough, rocky passage alongside the creek called Plum Run. Then the ground opens to the little valley at the base of Little Round Top. Across the valley from the hill, the huge boulders of Devil's Den crowd up.

You remember this place from quiet times. You're not ready for the scene of mayhem and terror that you and Avery Hill stumble into now.

Turn to page 47.

You can't share this crucial information with the general whose army has invaded your town. You've got to reach the Union lines and tell them what you know—that the hill called Little Round Top is their critical weak point.

"What are you thinking of?" General Lee asks.

"Oh . . . nothing."

"I think it is something." He studies you.

"No. Really. General Lee," you say, standing up, "I've told you all I know. It would really be great if I could go now. I'm . . . I'm worried about my family."

General Lee's face is grave. "We are all worried about our families," he says. "And our families are even more worried about us. I'm afraid this is war. I cannot let you go."

"What? You can't?"

"You have seen my headquarters, the position of our troops. What's more, I strongly suspect there is information that you have decided not to tell me. I cannot take the chance that you may share it with my enemy."

He knows! What's going to happen?

As if General Lee has heard your thought, he says, "Do not worry. You won't be harmed. But you must stay here in this camp tonight. Colonel Cole, the officer who brought you here, will see that you are fed and given a blanket. You'll be assigned a guard. It is most important that you not try to leave this camp tonight."

Now Lee stands up. "Thank you," he says, "for the information you have chosen to give."

Turn to page 91.

38

Before you stands a skinny girl about your age. She wears a clean print dress. The light color contrasts with her coal-dark arms, legs, and face. She is trembling.

This is no Union general, frightened of prison camp. This is someone with a greater fear.

"Lorena Solver," you whisper. "Why aren't you home?"

"They came there," she says. "They took my momma, my brother, my little sister, too. They're taking all of us—everyone they can catch. Back South. Into slavery."

"Rena, I—"

"I ain't goin'." She draws herself up straight, though she still shakes a little. "Rena Solver was born a free woman, and she's going to stay a free woman. Or die one."

Turn to page 29.

That night everything in town is quiet. At dawn you're down the stairs and about to run out the door.

"Wait!" your mother says. "Where are you going?"

"To meet up with Billy."

"I'd rather you stayed," she says. "I'm worried."

"I'll be back soon," you promise. And you're gone, running west toward Seminary Ridge.

Billy Bayley's farmhouse is just beyond the ridge. He's waiting for you.

"Any action?" you ask.

"None yet," he says. "But there were campfires all over, all night."

You run out to the open spread of land above town. To the west stands a long line of blue troops, facing the other way. They have a few cannons. Just back of their line stand some men with groups of horses, clutching the reins.

"That's the cavalry," says Billy.

"Let's climb," you say, pointing to an oak tree. "I want to see."

Billy nods.

Turn to page 46.

You decide to make a break for it.

Like a snake in slow motion, you slither loose from your blanket. You slide your eyes to one side. Your guard doesn't move.

You're worming your way toward a tree about six feet away. You move a few inches, then lie as if asleep. Move, then lie.

It seems to take hours.

Finally you're close. Taking a deep breath, you crawl quickly—then stop, your back against the tree. There's no sound.

Now: *run!*

As you dash into the darkness along Seminary Ridge, you hear feet shuffling behind you. Then clicking sounds. Now a voice shouts:

"You—stop there! You!"

Turn to page 50.

So far the Rebels have been the dashing winners of this war, and the Yankee bluecoats the bumbling losers. The Confederates have been outnumbered and outgunned, but they've won almost every battle.

Your father says slavery is evil, and you agree about that. But aren't the Rebels fighting for their homeland? So far, every single battle has been fought in the South.

It isn't easy to decide which side is right in this war. And up until now your imagination has been captured by all the stories you've heard about the ragged, reckless fighters under General Robert E. Lee.

"Climb a tree," the man says. "You'll get a sight."

Billy looks at you. "Let's go," he says.

"No. We'll climb into the cupola at the seminary."

"But won't your father be mad?" Your father teaches at the Lutheran Theological Seminary, a school for ministers nearby.

"Nobody's minding us today," you say. "Come on."

Turn to page 3.

In this backyard, you look around. No one seems to be watching. Casually you sidle over by the woodshed. It's low and built of rough planks, with a narrow door.

"They're gone," you whisper, staring straight ahead.

"Thank you," says a voice from the shed.

"Are you really a general?"

"Yes. I am Brigadier General Schimmelfennig. Division Commander, Seventy-fourth Pennsylvania Infantry."

"Well, you're in a woodshed now."

"Apparently so. Still, it is better than a prison camp."

"Is the battle lost?" you ask.

"Our soldiers have been ordered to regroup outside town," the general says. "But I cannot join them just now."

"I guess not," you say. "Wait here, okay?"

There's a haughty sniff from inside—then a sneeze.

"General, *don't sneeze!*"

"Sorry," says the voice.

Now what should you do?

Turn to page 62.

The coal chute leads from street level to the coal bin beside the big cellar stove. You climb over the dirty coal and look up. It ought to be just big enough.

"But it's filthy," your mother says.

"I've got no choice," you answer. With your father pushing up on your legs, you worm and scrunch upward until you can hook one hand around the top. You push open the hatch. It clatters to the street. You wait a second, then poke your head out. No one is there.

You're covered in coal dust, blackened from head to foot. You start up a side lane when you hear a voice behind you shout, "Hey! Hey—you! Stop!"

You run. There's a *crack,* and a bullet whistles by. The voice behind you cries, "Here, boys! Here's a slave!"

Turn to page 56.

You both scramble up. You climb out on a branch, push aside some leaves, and look out.

Beyond the thin line of blue cavalry, coming up the far side of the next ridge, are soldiers in gray—wave after wave after wave. They're not yet visible from the ground, but from your perch you see that thousands and thousands of Rebels are approaching. Marching in wide, orderly crowds, they fill the road and spread across the fields. Dust rises everywhere.

"Let's get out of here," Billy whispers. But before you can start down, the ground beneath you erupts in flame and smoke and thunders with explosions.

The battle has begun—and you're trapped in a tree.

Turn to page 72.

The area before you, leading to the base of Little Round Top, will be known after today as the Valley of Death. Already you see why.

Bloody and wounded Rebel soldiers are writhing among the big rocks. From up ahead where the ground opens comes smoke and roar and firing. The battle has passed through here and left dozens, maybe hundreds, of casualties. Men whose bodies are torn by ragged holes lie soaked in blood. One poor soldier with shattered legs pulls himself toward some sheltering rocks, like a lizard someone has stepped on. Others lie motionless.

"Come on!" shouts Hill, yanking at the stretcher.

With the other stretcher-bearers you begin moving among the rocks and bodies. You start loading those who are not too terribly wounded. You lift one soldier and he howls with pain. You almost drop him. But you don't. Your hands are sticky with blood. Once you get each wounded soldier loaded, you dash back to the shelter of the woods and simply unload him. That's all— no bandaging, no water. Then you run back toward the fighting.

For an hour you move back and forth at a steady run, ignoring the bullets that whiz up ahead. Steadily you move closer to the fighting, until you come out at the edge of the valley.

Looking up, you see the fight for Little Round Top has reached a crisis.

Turn to page 20.

You decide to share the crucial information with General Lee. You take a deep breath. "General Lee," you say, "there's a hill at the bottom of Cemetery Ridge." You sketch a rough circle.

Lee peers intently at your drawing. "Yes?"

"It's higher than the ridge. The trees have been cleared from its front."

Instantly the great general understands. "If we take this hill, we will command the whole Federal position," he says. "What is this hill called?"

"Little Round Top, sir."

"Hmm. And the ground around Little Round Top—what is it like?"

"In front of the hill is a little valley that's very rocky, General. Just across it lies a jumble of huge boulders that people call Devil's Den. Sometimes we play there."

The general looks at you. "Do you play soldier?"

"Yes, sir."

"Well, there will be real soldiers there tomorrow—a lot of them. We'll take that hill and win this battle."

Lee speaks to Colonel Cole. "Colonel, General Longstreet is bringing up the First Corps tonight. When he arrives, send him to see me right away."

"Of course, General." The colonel nods to you and smiles. Then he leaves the tent.

You're all alone with Robert E. Lee.

Turn to page 63.

That first boom was a Confederate signal gun. Seconds later the artillery opens up on the Rebel side—and the Yankees respond.

In an instant, Cemetery Ridge becomes a blasting, quaking, smoking, swirling chaos. From beside your wagon the crews rush to their guns and swing into a fast dance as they load, tamp, step back, and fire. Each shell launches in a roar of smoke and flame; the cannon jerks backward and then the crews swing back into the hot and smoke-swirled dance. The smoke blows over you, smelling acrid and nasty.

And the noise! These Union guns that launch the roaring, whistling shells are also the targets of the Rebel cannons—so explosive shells and solid cannonballs come whizzing, sailing, whirring, and whistling like crazed pigeons toward Cemetery Ridge. The explosions hit one after another, and more on top of those. Thunderous detonations pound at you two or three times a second. The ground shakes. Up blast geysers of dirt, rocks, and people.

Lee hopes to pound the Federal troops and gunners so hard they'll fall back, shell-shocked, when the great Southern charge begins. But as far as you can see the Union troops are hunkering down, flat to the earth behind their fences. And the gunners here are pounding right back.

"Rabbit!" It's McPherson. Through the smoke you see his pop-eyed face. "Git on the seat!" He leaps over and grabs the reins. You jump up beside him.

Turn to page 22.

50

You may have made a mistake, but you can't stop now. Got to keep going—run for those trees up ahead . . .

A *crack* explodes in the darkness behind you, then again and again. Something both warm and ice-cold hits your leg, and as you fall your back is punched hard. That's how it feels when the second minié ball hits. You thud onto the ground.

You're breathing hard. You can't turn over.

Shoes come pounding up. A hand gently turns you.

Staring up, you see a face, two faces. Now you're faintly surprised to see a gray-bearded man. As he bends toward you, the others draw away.

Slowly, the man shakes his head.

"Oh, what a sad shame is war," says Robert E. Lee. "What a terrible, terrible shame." He puts his hand on yours, and you understand the great, deep sadness in his brown eyes.

And now everything goes dark.

The End

From the cook's description you instantly recognize General George Gordon Meade, the Union commander. A thin-faced man with stringy hair and beard and droopy eyes, Meade seems gloomy and thoughtful. Around him stand a half dozen other top officers. Each man wears a long blue coat with a double row of brass buttons.

You can hardly believe you've come from Robert E. Lee's headquarters to General Meade's. You struggle to stay calm as you carry the bread platter around to the officers.

General Meade takes a slice without looking. He's talking to a handsome, tall officer with a dashing long mustache. You don't know it but this is General Winfield Scott Hancock, commander of the Union center and already one of the heroes of Gettysburg.

"Well, General," Hancock is saying, "the center is solid now—and I'm bringing up more troops every hour."

"Good," mumbles Meade, munching his bread. "Let's just hope I'm right."

"I believe you are," says Hancock. "Lee has hit us hard on both ends and failed. He'll try the center today."

Go on to the next page.

The center! Then Meade has guessed Lee's plan. If you can somehow get back to Lee, you could head off disaster for the Rebels. But *should* you? It's not your fight—even Lee said that. If he's going to make a colossal mistake, what can you do to stop him? Yet Lee's men have fought so bravely; you can't stand to think of them all dying on the long fields between you.

You look at your serving tray. It's empty.

Your brain churns as you walk back to the kitchen.

The cook takes your tray. He loads it with butter.

You stand there, staring at the butter.

"Well?" says the cook. "Go!"

Startled, you nod and step back out. It must be noon by now, or even a little after. Should you try to get away from here? Could you possibly reach the Southern lines in time?

Turn to page 104.

54

Seminary Ridge, long, low, and lined with oak trees, runs straight south from the building you are perched atop. Close by on your left sits the tidy town of brick homes and church spires. Gettysburg is the county seat, and roads converge here from all directions: from your state's capital of Harrisburg, from Baltimore and Washington, D.C.

Just beyond town is a hill with a new cemetery. From that hill a second straight ripple, Cemetery Ridge, also runs south. Below the town it faces across the farm fields toward Seminary Ridge. The two ridges are parallel, but Cemetery rises higher. At its far end are two rough hills: Little Round Top, its rocky face open to your view, and beyond it Big Round Top, covered in woods.

You watch the Federal cavalry emerge from Gettysburg and pass beneath your perch. Beyond Seminary Ridge they stop and begin setting up camp. You look beyond them and spot a column of men in tan or gray clothes coming this way.

You point. Billy nods. "There's Johnny Reb," he says. "Your heroes."

Are the Rebels your heroes? Sure, Lee's soldiers have bravely defended their homeland—but now they're in *your* territory.

If there's a big fight here, which side will you choose?

Turn to page 40.

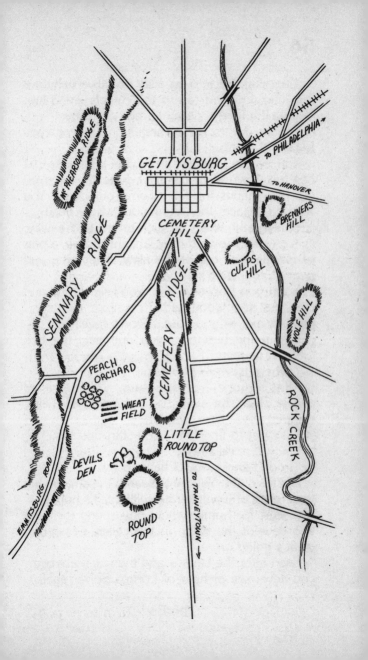

You scramble into an alley and dive behind a rain barrel. You listen to the Rebels searching. You wait a long time, until they go away.

You've got to do something. Suddenly you realize: the barrel!

You look in. The barrel is full of rainwater that has run down from the roof gutter above. You dip your hands in. They come out clean. You wash your face, then dunk your whole head.

Shaking the water off, you return to the alley. As you hustle toward the Garlachs' home, a pair of Rebels dash out of the alley. They stop and peer at you, then run past.

Soon you hop over the wood-slat fence and trot past the woodshed. "Evening, General," you whisper as you pass. "Don't sneeze."

But in the basement you find only the two Garlach women.

"Where is she?" you ask.

"She's gone," Anna says. "She waited awhile, but she was so frightened of being trapped down here, she left."

"I've got to find her." You start upstairs.

"How?" calls Anna.

"I don't know—but I have to try."

But it's night. You try to search the streets, but they're full of Confederate soldiers. It's hopeless. You start for home, where you spend the next two days of the battle in the cellar, wondering what's going on.

Even after the battle—and the war—are over, you never see or hear of Lorena Solver again.

The End

The houses open onto fenced-in fields. Confederate sharpshooters peek from the upstairs windows behind you. Ahead you can see bristling Union fortifications on Cemetery Hill. The night's fight for that hill has subsided, with the Federals still in control.

As you walk you wave the white flag and wait for a bullet to hit you. "Be confident," the colonel told you.

You hold your head up and walk steadily.

Turn to page 66.

58

Then the Rebel waves the pistol downward.

"They're in the cellar," he says. "Go join them. It's not safe up here."

You turn away, taking a deep breath. In the kitchen, you open the cellar door.

"Hello?"

"Oh," says your mother. "Thank heaven it's you!"

You go downstairs. A lamp is lit, and your father's and mother's faces flicker in the yellow light. Your mother holds your little sister.

"Where were you?" she asks. "We were so worried."

"I got trapped between the armies," you say. "A Rebel officer caught me after the battle, but he let me go."

"They seem to be decent folk—at least to civilians," your father agrees, nodding. He's a thoughtful man, a minister and a teacher who believes that war is wrong, but slavery is worse. "But the fighting, we hear, was brutal."

"It was awful—there's dead and wounded all over," you say. "What should we do?"

"Do?" your father frowns. "We'll stay here, where it's safe. Until the battle's over."

Your heart sinks.

"Father," you say, "Lorena Solver is hiding nearby. The Rebels took her family back to slavery. She's the only one they didn't catch. She needs me to help her get to the Union lines."

Your mother's breath catches. She looks at your father, and so do you. What will he say?

Turn to page 21.

At the clump of trees and the angle in the wall the Rebels start to pour over. The Yankees are breaking here—yet everywhere else along the line they have stopped the Confederates. Down the line, bluecoats fire fiercely into Rebel troops who are falling back; but here the men in gray surge ahead, their officers waving swords and working their mouths. You wish you could hear what they're saying.

Instead you turn, and again you're staggered by an awesome sight. Coming up the back side of Cemetery Ridge at a dead run are hundreds of Federal troops. Fresh reinforcements are hurtling at the battling, battered Confederates.

When they hit the fight, the new blue troops, dozens of ranks deep, are far too much. The Rebels have no reinforcements—Lee has thrown everything into one massive, heroic charge. In an immense, long rank his best men have marched across the open fields and into the fiercest fire the Yankees could deliver. They've almost broken the line, but now they're pounded back. The Rebel attack wavers, sags, and comes apart.

Dozens of men in gray are down. Those still on their feet turn, fighting as they stagger back. The fields are covered with the running, the limping, the dead, and the dying. Slowly, sadly, thousands of men struggle to drag themselves and their wounded comrades in a vast, bloody crowd back to Seminary Ridge.

Pickett's Charge has failed.

Turn to page 80.

You're bending toward a young soldier in gray who's been badly wounded in the legs. He sips through cracked lips and smiles a little as his head sags back on the ground. Then he nods.

You look up to see legs all around you.

You rise quickly, but the squad of Confederates has you surrounded. Lorena looks up and freezes.

"You can go," a soldier says to you. "You," he says to Lorena, "come with us."

She looks at you. Her eyes are wide with terror.

You look past the soldiers and see the Rebel surgeon. "You!" you say angrily. "You told!"

He shrugs. "Of course I did," he says.

"How can you help these men and then send *her* into slavery?"

"Well," he says, looking at the wounded, "these are people."

"So? What's she?"

"Why," he says, "that's a slave."

A soldier shoves you away with his rifle butt. Two of them grab Lorena by the arms. She just stares with frozen eyes as they drag her back toward the Confederate lines. You're left standing there, wondering how one person could look at another and not see a human being.

Now you understand what this war's about. And now, at last, you know which side you're on.

The End

You move to the back porch of a house near the woodshed. Slowly you push open the door, but you see no light, hear no sound.

"Hello? Anna? Mrs. Garlach?"

A teenage girl, Anna Garlach, lives here with her mother. Her father is off fighting in the war. You push the cellar door open a crack.

"Hello?"

There's silence—but something tells you someone is down there. You step down the creaking wood stairs.

It's dim down here. The only light comes in through the high, narrow cellar windows. As your eyes grow used to the murk, you see three figures cowering in a corner.

"Anna? Is that you? It's only me."

"Oh!" In the shadows Anna Garlach stands and wipes her hands nervously. "We didn't know. We're afraid the soldiers will come."

"I know." You recognize Anna's mother, but the third figure is small and dark. You don't know who it is.

"Anna, there's a general in your woodshed."

"A *what?* Who?"

"I can't say his name, but he's a Federal general. The Rebs were after him. He's got to stay there. Will you look out for him?"

"Yes—we'll try. But you've got to look after someone, too."

You don't understand. But now Anna gestures toward the corner and the third, shadowy form steps forward.

Turn to page 38.

"Shall I go, General Lee?" you ask.

"No," he says. "Stay and tell me more. There's a lot I must learn, and quickly. Besides," he says, his deep eyes softening, "I've missed the companionship of young people."

And so you stay. Carefully you describe the countryside around Gettysburg. After a while, Lee asks about your family. You tell him they live in town—and that you're worried.

"Are they safe?" you ask. "I mean, from your soldiers."

Lee nods. "I have ordered my men to treat all civilians with respect," he says. "Still, I will send a message to your family. They'll be told that you are safe behind Confederate lines." He asks your address and gives the message to an orderly.

"Now," says Lee, "my camp is yours for the night. Colonel Cole will see that you are fed and given a blanket. You must remain under guard."

You swallow. "Under . . . guard?"

"Yes," Lee says. "You know the critical element of our plans for tomorrow's attack. That information must stay here. Please," he adds, "do not try to leave this camp."

As an orderly leads you out of Lee's tent, you wonder—once the battle is over, will they let you go?

Turn to page 91.

"All right," you tell Lorena. "I'll try."

Lorena Solver is smart and nervy. The only difference between you and her right now is that if the Confederates catch Rena, they'll ship her into slavery—even though she was born here, as free as you. You don't know what they'll do to you.

"The general says the Federal troops are gathering on the other side of town," you say.

"Who is this general?" Rena demands. "How's he know?"

"His name is Shimmering Penny or something. He's in the woodshed."

"Oh, *that's* how he knows!" Her eyes flash.

"Listen, Lorena, it makes sense. There are hills down Baltimore Street, just past town—good hills and Cemetery Ridge, too. The Federals could make a stand."

"So that's all we've got to do—get a few blocks down Baltimore Street?"

"It won't be that easy."

"I *know* it won't be easy. This whole town is full of Southern devils. They're searching for bluecoats—and for us," the black girl says.

"You could wrap Lorena in a blanket," Anna suggests. "Pretend she's sick."

"You could hide her under a wheelbarrow of potatoes," offers Mrs. Garlach.

"But if they're searching, they'll check," you answer. "No, I think we should head backward—*away* from the Union lines. Back where they fought today."

Turn to page 76.

Several hours pass, but General Lee just sits there. He speaks to you only once.

"I've sent General Longstreet's First Corps into the woods down below us," he says. "Our scouts tell us there are no Union troops on the hill down there. Meanwhile, I've ordered General Ewell's Second Corps to attack the two hills above town—mostly to divert the Yankees. After both attacks have begun and the Yankees have rushed their troops to both ends, we'll send the Third Corps right at the center of Cemetery Ridge. We'll break through."

"What's on the other side, General?"

He stares ahead. "Washington, D.C. Baltimore. Philadelphia. Victory," says Lee.

The day drags on in suspense. Then, in midafternoon, Confederate cannons open up on your right. After their heavy thunder begins, the Rebel artillery up close to town starts firing, too.

The ground shudders with roars and crashes. Now the Federals answer with *their* cannons—and the whole world is in uproar.

All along both lines, gray smoke billows up and catapults forward. The air is dense with metal, with heavy flying shells. They give off strange whirring and whistling sounds—then crashing and thunderous shaking, and terrible explosions.

Lee turns to you.

"Get to safety," he says.

Safety? *Where?*

Turn to page 15.

Along the Taneytown Road at the base of Cemetery Hill, a sentry steps from behind a barricade of piled logs and fence posts.

"What's your purpose?"

"Bread—for the wounded," you say, holding up the bag. The sentry opens the bag and looks in. Deeply, dreamily, he inhales the warm scent.

You whisper, "Like one?"

He looks around. "Quickly," he says. You slip him a loaf. He sticks it in his dark blue jacket and stands aside.

The road runs in back of Cemetery Ridge. You walk into a throng of activity that grows and grows—dozens of carts and wagons, horses pulling cannons, and marching troops many ranks deep. The Federals have so much more of everything.

You turn and start to climb the ridge, toward the center of the Union line.

"Stop," a voice commands. A sharp-faced rifleman steps up. "Where do you think you're going?"

You think fast. "There—the Widow Leister's house," you say, pointing to a little farm cottage up ahead. "I've got bread for the . . ."

"Yes, the generals," he says, sighing heavily. "Who else gets good bread? I'll take you there."

The *generals?*

Turn to page 89.

You and Billy make it a few hundred feet. But the firing around you grows too intense. You see a barn with high stone walls. "In here!" you shout. Billy is already diving through the door.

Inside are horses and pigs, restless and frightened. You and Billy crouch low and hide. Pieces of the barn are blown in. Amid the explosions and the dense clamor of firing, you hear footsteps running—first this way, then that. Afraid to look out, you've got no idea who's winning the fight.

Finally, late in the day, the firing eases. You hear men outside. Lots of men. You don't know who they are.

"Let's have a look," you tell Billy.

"I'm scared. You look," he says.

"Okay," you say.

You open the big barn door, step outside—and freeze.

The farm, the open land, everyplace you can see is covered with bodies. Most are bluecoated bodies. Some of them move. Many don't. But that's not the worst. Glancing toward Gettysburg, you see the Confederate army on the run, charging at your hometown.

"Please put your hands up," says a soft Southern voice.

Turn to page 114.

It's as if your senses are overwhelmed and decide to just shut down. You're in a dark, dreamless sleep. The noise of the great bombardment is gone.

How long you stay this way, you don't know. Opening your eyes, you see McPherson beside you. Maybe he's just sleeping, too.

The bombardment must have ended. It's quiet. In fact, apart from a funny kind of ringing in your ears, everything is silent. Could the battle be over?

You stand and look down at McPherson. Something about him isn't right. You kneel and listen to his chest. It's silent. His face is cold.

You rip open his shirt. There's a thin wound in his chest. Turning him over, you see where the piece of sharp metal shot into his back, so sharp and hard it kept going right out the other side.

McPherson is dead.

You kneel by him awhile, just staring. You can hardly believe it. But now men are running past you. You look up to see soldiers, their blue coats flying open—they're leaping down the ridge and running past you. Their mouths are wide open. You wonder why there's no sound.

You struggle to push forward, to get up the slope the men are leaving. You reach the crest and just stand there, stunned by what you see.

Turn to page 34.

"Move over!" shouts Avery Hill. You and he huddle together while the Federal minié balls whine, whistle, and ricochet.

After several endless minutes, the firing eases. The Confederates have mostly run into the woods to regroup. You don't think they'll attack again here. You can see more and more Union forces coming onto Little Round Top, fortifying their hold. Cannons are moving in, and troops are taking cover behind rocks and trees.

Behind you, a shot rings out. You look back just as a gray-uniformed soldier ducks behind the massive rocks of Devil's Den. From Little Round Top a spasm of firing responds. The bullets ping off the rocks behind you.

"It'll be a set-to of sharpshooters from now on," says Hill. "Come on."

"Where?"

"Out there." He jerks his thumb toward the Valley of Death at the base of the hill. You peer over the rock. The rough ground is humped and carpeted with men in awful condition—gray and blue men both.

"The sharpshooters won't fire at us," he assures you.

You swallow. "Do we only bring in the Rebels?"

Avery Hill shakes his head. "No," he says. "We get everyone we can reach. Once a soldier is down, he's just a person again."

Turn to page 84.

The Federals are massing on the two hills at the top of Cemetery Ridge. But at the *bottom* are more hills—Little and Big Round Top. Little Round Top, the closer one, looms right over the Union positions—and lately a farmer has cleared the trees from its rocky face. From that open hilltop, Confederate cannons could blast the Federal army right out of the war.

Right now you may be the only one who knows this key to victory in the Battle of Gettysburg. Should you tell General Lee what you know? He'll probably find out anyway, but maybe not soon enough to beat the Federals to Little Round Top.

You could play a huge part in history—maybe. And perhaps the Confederates deserve to win this war. Now that you've met such impressive men as General Lee and Colonel Cole, you wonder again if their cause could be so wrong.

Yet you and your family are Northerners. If the South wins, what will it do to your homeland? What will happen to your family?

Something about General Lee makes you want to help him. But you could also try to reach the Union leaders, and tell them instead.

General Lee is watching you. He can tell there's something on your mind. Should you tell him the secret to victory?

If you tell Lee about Little Round Top, turn to page 48.

If you try to reach the Union leaders instead, turn to page 37.

72

The air rattles with the clatter of muskets firing. Your tree shudders as cannons blast. Dark smoke swirls around, stabbed with flaming darts. Men shout; somebody screams. Shot thuds into the trunk beneath your feet.

"We've got to get out of this!" Billy shouts.

You have no idea what's happening. You can't see. You're not sure what to do. You don't think this line of cavalry can hold off all those Confederates. But when the smoke swirls off, the bluecoats are still there, still firing. And the huge masses of Rebels are coming on.

"They're aiming beneath us—we're safer up here," you tell Billy. "Let's just watch awhile."

The battle builds, fiercer and louder. You see a bluecoat blown backward. Other Federals lie motionless on the ground. A shot rips off a branch just a few feet away. You really could be killed!

"Let's go!" you shout. "Drop and run to town."

Turn to page 7.

You decide to stay and see what you can learn here inside the Union headquarters. It's not yet noon. Lee's attack is planned for midafternoon. You only hope you've got enough time.

You cut the loaves into slices. The cook returns. "Good," he grunts. He gives you some onions to chop for the officers' lunch.

"So," you say to the cook as you chop, "what's General Meade like?"

The cook chuckles. "He's a goggle-eyed old snapping turtle—says so himself. But I'd say General Meade is doing right well, this being the biggest battle of the war, and his first in command."

"This is his *first* battle?"

"In command, yes. Lincoln put him in charge just a few days ago. Surprised a lot of people. Meade might not be the shining leader type—he's more like a gloomy old professor. But he's smart. And he's made the right moves so far."

This might be your chance. "What about today?" you ask. "Is he ready for the Rebels today?"

The cook's eyes narrow. "How should I know? You ask too many questions. When you're serving the officers, keep your lips shut. Understand?"

Go on to the next page.

"Ah . . . okay. I'm going to serve the officers?"

"That's right. It's a good thing you came along. Here." He hands you a platter of bread. "The officers have gathered in the yard. Go serve them. When the tray is empty, come back."

You step outside—into the midst of the Union high command.

Turn to page 52.

Lorena claps her hands on her hips. "You're crazy," she says. "I always suspected it."

"No—listen. It's our only chance. The Rebel soldiers are all crowded in the middle of town and down Baltimore Street where they chased the Federals," you explain. "At the back end of town it's quiet. I've just come from there. When you get past the houses, there's nothing but dead and wounded out there. We'll get into the fields and sneak across till we see the Federal campfires."

Lorena frowns. "How do we get out of town?"

"Backyards. We only have to go a little ways."

"Okay," she says. "Let's go."

"First you got to change. That dress is too bright."

"Wait one minute," says Anna Garlach. She runs upstairs and comes back with jeans, a dark, long shirt, and a baggy cap.

"These are Father's," she says. Lorena puts them on. They hang loose and shapeless, hiding your dark-skinned friend inside.

"Perfect," you say.

A moment later you're poking your head out the back door.

"Let's go," you whisper. You boost Lorena over the plank fence. You only hope there's no one on the other side.

Turn to page 92.

You decide not to risk an escape.

The next morning, July 2, you expect a battle —but nothing happens. No battle, that is. Yet all around you, after they've eaten breakfast and doused their campfires, Rebel troops start to move. You stay in Lee's camp as officers come and go. Then Lee sends for you again.

At the edge of his camp the general sits on a stump. He gazes out from the trees of Seminary Ridge across the gold wheat fields that slope gently upward toward distant Cemetery Ridge. It's a warm day. The sun pokes through the clouds.

You wonder if Lee knows you're here. He seems deep in thought. But now he points to the opposing ridge, higher and almost a mile away. He says, "See what the sun catches up there?"

You look—and your breath skips. All across Cemetery Ridge you can see light glinting off shiny objects. From one end to the other, along the far-off stone walls and gleaming through the clumps of trees, the sunlight strikes metal.

"They're all there," says Lee. "The whole Army of the Potomac. They fortified the entire position in the night. This is going to be a frightful day. But we'll drive them off those heights— I'm sure of it. My men can do anything."

Anything? The Rebels' bravery is legendary, and Lee's eyes are glittering. But you look at those heights and wonder. This time, is it possible that Robert E. Lee could be wrong?

Turn to page 65.

The tracks cut over to Washington Street—which leads into a crowded, poorer part of Gettysburg, a jumble of tiny houses, sheds, and back alleys. To you this has always been the most interesting part of town. A lot of black people live here. Many of them, or their parents, escaped slavery years ago. Gettysburg lies only about ten miles from the Mason-Dixon Line, the division between slave and free states.

Right now you don't see anyone, black or white.

You climb over plank fences, crossing backyards. You're not far from home when you hear pounding feet, then voices and a gun firing.

A man dashes into this backyard. He has a beard and a blue coat with one star on each shoulder patch. A Union general!

You hear a crowd coming. You know right away the general's about to be captured, and you've got to help.

You dash to the back fence and cup your hands. "Quick," you whisper. The general nods and puts one boot into your hands.

"On the other side is a woodshed," you say. He nods. You heave up, and the general scrambles over, half a breath before a dozen Rebel soldiers charge into the yard.

You straighten calmly. The men scan the tiny yard. One places his gun barrel against your nose.

"Tell where he went," he says. "Or I'll kill you."

Turn to page 106.

To you it all seems kind of dreamlike, because there is no sound. As you turn and start to walk down the ridge, you suddenly realize why. Those explosions destroyed your hearing. There is plenty of sound, but you can't hear it. You are deaf.

In the years to come, you become a great writer and scholar of the battle. A fine historian, you tell the tale of Gettysburg: how close the South came to victory at Little Round Top on the second day, and again the next day at the angle in the wall on Cemetery Ridge.

You tell how Robert E. Lee's great faith in his troops finally, on that third day, pushed them to a charge that could not succeed—and how afterward the Rebel army was never the same. Forced to end its invasion and retreat across the Potomac River, the Army of Northern Virginia fought on for two more years, dwindling in strength until finally, on April 9, 1865, Lee surrendered to General Ulysses S. Grant at a little courthouse in Virginia called Appomattox.

Turn to page 99.

Terror-stricken, you run from the Valley of Death with the fleeing Confederates. You half-expect Hill to chase you down and grab you, but he doesn't. You never see him again.

You run past the wounded men you've laid among the trees without stopping. You stumble through the woods. All around you men are doing the same. But you see officers moving among the soldiers, gathering them into groups again. The Rebel fighting units are re-forming.

You keep forging through the woods until you reach the road that runs along Seminary Ridge. It's late in the day and the storm of battle is fading from the fields, woods, and orchards between enemy lines. Exhausted and bloody soldiers return from those fights, some in organized units, others singly and in ragged groups. More stretcher-bearers bring in the wounded. You dodge through all the movement, shouting, and confusion. You know where you're going.

You reach Lee's headquarters. Incredibly, the general is still sitting on the stump.

The sentry recognizes you. He nods. Quietly, you approach the general.

"General Lee," you say, "It's—it's awful."

He nods and turns to you. "Yes," he says. "It's always awful. We hit them hard today, and we almost broke them in several places. Tomorrow we *will* break them—if we hit them with everything, right there."

He points straight ahead, toward the very center of Cemetery Ridge.

Turn to page 112.

82

It's almost twelve. Lee's attack is planned for midafternoon. You've got to try for a look at the Union defenses.

You sidle to the back door. You glance out. No one's looking. You leave the house and begin walking quickly uphill.

The day is heating up. All around you on this back side of Cemetery Ridge there is urgent movement. Crowds of blue soldiers hurry past, going up the slope and coming back down. Horses draw heavy wagons that creak loudly.

"Hey, you—jump aside!" someone yells behind you. You turn and leap just as two huge horses haul a wagon past. The red-faced driver cracks his whip and curses. Foam sprays from the horses' mouths, so close it wets your face.

"Gettin' crushed by an artillery wagon is no way to die, youngster!" yells the driver, grinning at you as he passes.

On tiptoe you strain to peek in the wagon. You see row after row of big metal balls.

You've got an idea. In a second you're running alongside the driver.

"Can you use a hand?" you shout.

"Are you crazy?" the man yells. "Hightail it out of here—they're planning on *firing* these things!" He has flaming red hair, and sweat soaks his undershirt.

"No," you insist, "I want to help."

The driver looks around. "Some people got no sense," he growls. And he leans down to offer you a huge, red-freckled hand.

Turn to page 88.

You're just a kid—this isn't your war. Just as you decide to run for Billy Bayley's farmhouse, a shell explodes much too close. The air detonates, and you're sent sprawling.

But you're okay. Smoke is everywhere. You don't even look for the stretcher; you just get up and run the other way.

You dash past stone walls, fields, trees, even sprawled bodies—dead men still lying where they fell yesterday. It's a blur, and none of it stops you. As you sprint farther into the fields behind Seminary Ridge, the roar and crash of artillery fades.

You see Billy's house. It's still there. You run through the remains of the old fencing. There are no animals anywhere. And where are the people?

You throw open the kitchen door. Inside, in the shadows, are two figures. You recognize one.

"Billy!"

Then you peer more closely at the other. You stop dead when you see the gray uniform.

Have you been captured again?

Turn to page 31.

You're scared, but you follow Hill, gripping your end of the stretcher. Sure enough, nobody fires. Crouching, you reach a wounded Rebel. His jacket is soaked in blood. He wheezes.

"Got to leave him," Hill says. "He's shot in the chest, poor fellow. He can't make it."

And so it has to be. You and Hill move among the dead and the dying, looking for those who might survive. One after another you load them onto your bloody stretcher. You bring them through the rocks along Plum Rum back toward the woods. Just inside the trees you lay them down. Other stretcher-bearers do the same. The woods are filling up with wounded men.

"What happens to them?" you ask Hill.

"Ambulance wagons'll come. . . I hope."

Toward dark, exhausted, you finally slump against a tree.

"Stay with these men," Hill says. "Do what you can for them."

"With what?" you ask. "I've got nothing."

Hill nods. "I know. I'll try to fetch some water." He stops. "By the way, that was a brave thing you did. Staying to help, I mean. I know you thought about running."

"You did?"

"Sure. Everyone does. But you stayed. Some of these men will survive because of you."

He goes off. The men around you moan, cry, and struggle for breath. In the dimness, you can't tell who wears blue and who wears gray. Hill was right. It doesn't matter anymore.

Turn to page 19.

You can save this one life—or at least you can try.

You drop to one knee and shove both palms down on McPherson's wound, pressing with your whole body. In a few minutes the blood slows to an ooze. The big man pulls off his shirt and rips it with his teeth, making a bandage. You wrap it snugly around his leg.

You lean back. "I think it's going to be okay," you say.

A blast nearby flings you down. You cover your head. Looking up, you see McPherson is pale but grinning.

"Let's get to it, Rabbit!" He rises to his feet, staggering.

"What are you doing?" you shout through the turmoil.

"Back to work. Where's the wagon?"

"This time *you're* crazy," you shout. "The wagon's gone—it got splintered!"

"The horses?"

"They ran."

"Got to get them—got to find them . . ." McPherson lurches off uphill. He's acting strangely.

"Hey," you shout. "Wrong way!" But he's staggering up the ridge. You run after him, shouting.

Go on to the next page.

Amid the chaos you grab at the big man. "Mc-Pherson—the horses ran down that way. We've got to go that way!" He stares vaguely at you. What's wrong with him?

At that moment explosions detonate on both sides, and then one so close behind you that you shove the big man down and fling yourself after him. Stunned by the concussions, you hug the dirt and feel yourself slipping, falling into some strange daze.

Turn to page 69.

From the wagon seat you can see units of blue infantry marching up on the ridge.

"Name's McPherson," the big driver says. "What in consarnation are you doing here?"

"I brought some bread for the troops," you say. "I wanted to see—before the battle starts."

"Well, you haven't got the sense of a rabbit," McPherson says. "But I suppose it *is* a sight. Here—take a good look."

The wagon draws onto the ridgetop. You stand on the footboard to look up and down.

What you see is thousands of Union troops— and cannons, cannons, cannons.

There are dozens—more than a hundred—of the heavy guns. At every one, blue crews stand ready, or busily stack shells and cannonballs from wagons and two-wheeled caissons. Along the ridge crest behind every inch of fence are blue soldiers. They peer across the thousand– plus yards of rolling wheat toward Seminary Ridge. From down in the field you hear crack- ling; little scuds of smoke rise as Union and Con- federate advance pickets fire at each other.

"Boy," you say. "I guess you're ready."

"Ought to be—been *gettin'* ready all night and all day," McPherson answers. "I guess the generals figure Johnny Reb'll come straight at us today. If he did, I think he'd be even crazier than you are, Rabbit."

Turn to page 18.

The Federal rifleman leads you to the white cottage partway up Cemetery Ridge. Outside are tied several well-groomed horses. The soldier raps on the back door. A stocky man in rolled-up shirtsleeves and a dirty apron opens it.

"Here's a delivery for you," says the soldier.

The stocky man looks at you and at the bread. "What's that?"

"Bread," you say. "From town. For the . . . the generals."

"From town?" For a moment the man peers at you, puzzled. Then he shrugs. "Well! A sack of bread will do just fine. Come in—I can use you."

"But . . ."

"Go on," says the soldier, and he gives you a little push. "Out here's no place for a youngster."

Turn to page 6.

You're a prisoner in the Confederate camp. What did Lee mean when he warned you not to try leaving here tonight? And if you do leave—or if the Rebels let you go after the battle—will you be branded a traitor at home?

Your mind is awhirl. But you try to stay calm. Colonel Cole, gentlemanly as always, assigns a lean, mustached soldier in a tan jacket and tattered hat to guard you. The soldier brings you food—a tin plate with some hard, flat things under thick brown molasses.

"What is this stuff?"

"That's hardtack," says the soldier. He grins. "Flour-and-water biscuits—been eatin' 'em for three years. Taste like their name, don't they?"

You try to chew the hardtack.

"Tastes like a sawdusty old board," you say.

His grin widens. "You're lucky," he says. "We don't usually git m'lasses with it."

As night falls, officers gather at Lee's tent—you see several who look like generals, with long double-buttoned coats. Their faces are very serious. But around you the troops at their campfires break into laughter, jovial talk, and singing. You know many of the songs by heart. They're American songs.

You ask your guard, "Do they know they're going into battle tomorrow?"

"Sure they do," he says softly.

"Oh." You hug your knees to your chest.

An idea is stirring in your head. Will it be possible, later—much later—to escape?

Turn to page 14.

The noise of the Southern troops fades behind you. These backyards are deserted. In a few minutes you two are at the edge of town. You hunker down behind a shed, looking out at the fence-broken fields where the armies battled earlier today.

In the moonlight, the ground is scattered with dark shapes. Wrecked wagons stick sideways into the air. Dead horses lie alongside. The air is ghostly with the moans, cries, and wails of the wounded.

Lorena turns wide-eyed to you. "Can't anyone help them?"

"Some are," you answer, pointing. Out in the pale light stands a boxy wagon. Two figures are moving among the casualties. You see them stooping over those on the ground.

"Over this way," you say, taking Lorena's hand. "Let's go."

Stooping low, you scuttle alongside the battlefield. You're heading toward the wide, open farm fields that lie ahead, rolling south of town between Seminary and Cemetery ridges.

But a voice says, "Hey—you two! Can y'all hold on a second?"

Lorena's head whips around. "It's one of those helping people," she says. "Should we stop?"

Go on to the next page.

"No! He's a Southerner," you whisper. "Let's run for it."

"But people who help the wounded don't send folks to slavery."

"We don't *know* that."

"Well," she says, "should we see what he wants, or run?"

If you run and the Southerner is armed, you could be shot. But if you stay, you could be caught. What should you do?

If you start to run, turn to page 102.

If you stay, turn to page 32.

You've got to get away from here—if you stay you'll both be killed. You hope McPherson will make it somehow. You start to run. But you don't get far.

You don't hear the blast or feel everything go black. But when you open your eyes, everything is different.

You blink. It's night. And all is quiet.

You push up on your elbow—your head throbs something awful. You raise your hand and tenderly feel an egg-sized lump.

Above, the moon and stars are clouding over. It might rain soon. You stand up and climb the ridge. You can hardly believe the view.

The moon lights the long, wide, sloping field. The wheat is trampled flat and littered as far as you can see with bodies. Hundreds and hundreds of men—Rebel soldiers, most of them dead—are strewn about like tossed and forgotten rag dolls. Some of the wounded beg for help. Among them people move, giving drinks, loading men onto stretchers, piling the dead onto carts.

You can see that the Rebels have failed. It must have been an enormous charge, a huge fight, a terrible failure. Across the field, against the trees on Seminary Ridge, you can see men on horseback. Is one of them General Lee? You wonder how he must feel right now.

It starts to rain. You turn away from the field. The battle, you know, is over. And something tells you the Southern cause is lost.

The End

You stare at General Lee. Your throat is dry.

"What do you mean, rely on me?"

"Our charge is planned for the middle of tomorrow afternoon," Lee says. "I'd like you to leave this camp early tomorrow morning. Walk through town and cross the Union lines. We'll provide you with a sackload of bread to carry. If you're stopped, say you're bringing the bread to the troops. Get behind Cemetery Ridge. See how many troops are there. Then come back and tell me."

"But . . ."

"I know you're not a Southerner—this isn't your cause," Lee says kindly. "But if I send all my infantry against a Union line that's heavily defended, thousands upon thousands of men on both sides will die. I am the commander here—if there is a chance at victory, I must attack. But if there is no chance, we need not waste so many fine young lives. You can answer this question for me. Will you do it?"

For a long moment you stare at the ground. Will you do what Lee asks?

Turn to page 24.

You lift the stretcher and start to run. A couple of seconds later a shell plows into the earth not far from where you were standing and explodes. You're thrown hard to the ground. But you get up, grab the stretcher, and take off after Avery Hill and his drummers.

You wonder what you'll do with the wounded. Will you have to go right into Yankee fire? *Can you do that?*

Down Seminary Ridge you run, past an artillery battery that rages here in the trees. Back of the ridge an infantry unit sprawls on the grass, waiting.

You run until you're exhausted, heavy-footed and sweating. Your hands ache as they grip the stretcher, and your hip is sore from being banged. Below the ridge your group swings into dense woods. Ahead you see Rebel soldiers. You know you're coming toward the Round Tops.

Your group stops. In a few minutes, the awful bombardment subsides. Now there's a long, waiting silence.

It's broken by a stirring of leaves. The soldiers are moving. From everywhere in the woods around you rises a weird, high-pitched shrieking and howling, like men gone crazy.

You're hearing the famous Rebel Yell. The Confederates are attacking.

Turn to page 36.

At midmorning on Friday, July 3, clouds are clearing and the day is getting warm. Almost no townspeople are in the streets of Gettysburg— only Rebel soldiers, moving to and fro. You see wounded being carried into homes. You're accompanied by Colonel Cole, the gentlemanly officer from Lee's staff who first captured you. You're carrying a bumpy burlap sack.

You're very worried that someone who knows you will see you with this Rebel officer. When you were behind Confederate lines and with the great Robert E. Lee, this all seemed exciting— but now you realize you're actually aiding the enemy. Isn't this a crime? If you're spotted, will they hang you?

Down your back runs a trickle of icy sweat.

But the townspeople must be hiding in their homes, or they've fled town. In the bustle of troops and others, you pass unnoticed—you hope.

Near the edge of town, Colonel Cole stands aside. "Good luck," he says. He hands you a piece of white cloth tied to a stick.

"But . . . what if someone shoots me?"

"Just remember what to say and do. Be brave. You could be saving many lives."

"Or losing mine," you mutter.

You walk to the edge of town. Nervously you raise the white flag as you step out into no-man's-land, the space between the two armies.

Turn to page 57.

But in years to come it's Gettysburg that Americans will remember most. More than fifty thousand men—almost one out of every three soldiers who came to Gettysburg—were killed, wounded, or captured here. And the place called the Bloody Angle, where you stood and watched, will always be known as the high tide of the Confederacy. Here the Rebels came closest to winning the Civil War.

Could you have stopped the charge before it began? You really don't think so. But you'll never know for sure.

The End

Four months pass. For the people of Gettysburg these four months are harder, in many ways, than the awful three days of war. After he is stopped on the second day and defeated on the third, Robert E. Lee turns his battered army back toward Virginia. The Federals follow. The twenty-four hundred people of Gettysburg are left to cope, as best they can, with the thousands on thousands of wounded, dead, and dying men that the armies leave behind.

For weeks you and Lorena work amid the terrible sights and sounds and the sickening smell that's everywhere in Gettysburg. Just about every house, church, and hall hangs out a little red flag to indicate it has been turned into a makeshift hospital. It is weeks before you get a day's rest, or enough to eat, or a break from the nightmarish suffering all around.

Gradually the wounded who survive are taken away to real hospitals. Body by body, crews bury the dead. They are under the ground everywhere in Gettysburg, it seems—in the fields, in the woods, beneath trees, and in the brand new National Cemetery.

On this November day a huge crowd covers that cemetery, here to watch its official dedication. From the midst of the throng you make your way outward until you spot Lorena at the edge. She's bouncing on tiptoes.

"Well?" she asks. "What did he say?"

"Which one?"

"The *president,* you dunderhead!"

Turn to page 116.

"Let's run for it," you whisper.

"Hey!" the voice yells. "Wait!"

You and Rena run hand in hand, leaving behind the trampled ground, the broken fences, and the casualties. Now you're in soft, high wheat fields. The moon shines on the grain.

You stop a moment. You look back at the dark trees of Seminary Ridge. You can see campfires.

"Those are the Rebs," you say to Lorena.

"So, then"—she points the other way, up ahead—"are those the Yankees?"

Ahead the long fields slope steadily toward higher ground. Up there is Cemetery Ridge. You can see little fires there, too.

"Yep. Looks like they made it," you say.

"The Yankees have the higher ground," Lorena says.

"Looks that way. Let's go."

You start to push across the fields. But there's one thing you don't know about Civil War armies.

When the infantries of this war face each other, each side sends out pickets—soldiers who take cover out in front of their side and lay low, keeping an eye on the enemy, shooting now and then.

Three figures rise from the tall grass.

Go on to the next page.

"What you two doin' here?" a soldier demands. You and Lorena have walked into a nest of Confederate pickets.

Beneath her baggy cap, Lorena lifts her eyebrows at you. They haven't seen that she's black —yet.

You know Lorena's going to run for it. Should you run with her—or throw yourself at the Rebels? That might gain Rena a few seconds. Either way might get you killed.

*If you run with Rena,
turn to page 26.*

*If you throw yourself at the soldiers to
give her time, turn to page 33.*

It's actually one o'clock as you begin to pass around the butter. Both the Union and Rebel-held ridges have been silent. But now a single gun sounds from Seminary Ridge.

You don't know it but you've just heard the signal gun for the Confederate artillery. They're starting what will be, over the next two hours, the most massive two-way artillery bombardment ever mounted so far in history—an overwhelming thunderstorm of shells from both sides.

There's a lot of roaring from the other side. One of the first shells from the Confederate batteries comes whistling over the Union front lines. It homes in on the yard of Meade's headquarters. As you are offering butter to the Federal generals, the shell obliterates you.

In years to come, historians of Gettysburg will retell the story of General Meade's "orderly" who was hit by one of the first shells in the Rebels' great bombardment on the third day. But no one knows the victim was really you. And no one ever learns what happened to you. To your grieving family—just like those of thousands of other Civil War casualties—it's as if you just disappeared.

The End

You glance sideways, down the long barrel. The Rebel's face is blackened from gunpowder. His eyes glitter.

"I mean it," he says. "Tell."

You shiver. "All right. He climbed that fence." You point to a fence across the yard.

"Go look," the Rebel tells the others. One scrawny man pulls himself up. He peers this way and that. You're sure this is the end; they'll discover your ruse.

But the soldier yells, "There's a bluecoat! I see him!"

The rifle drops from your face.

"Git!" the Rebel orders you. You hop over the fence—the way the general really went. You hear the Rebels clamber over and pound off noisily the wrong way. You wonder who they saw.

Turn to page 43.

"The Army of the Potomac gave us a hard fight today," Robert E. Lee says, "and I expect a harder one tomorrow."

"They've regrouped, then, General?" asks the officer who brought you here.

"Yes, Colonel Cole," says Lee. He spreads a sheet of paper on the rough table. You expect to see a map, but it's blank.

"As you know, the Federal troops have retreated through town," says Lee. "They've taken a new position on some high ground just beyond Gettysburg. I'm told there are two hills there, and another ridge. Is that right?"

"Why, yes," you say. "Cemetery Ridge."

Lee motions at the big sheet of paper. He hands you a pencil.

"Usually my cavalry tells me the lay of the land," he says. "But I haven't seen my cavalry for days. No one can tell me where they are. Please sketch these hills and ridges. Draw the map for the Battle of Gettysburg."

You stare at Lee's hand, holding out the pencil. Can you do this? Is it right? You're trembling as you look up into his eyes.

At once you know why this man is a great commander. Somehow his deep brown eyes tell you that *this must be done*. The strength of Lee's will is so overwhelming that your hand reaches for the pencil and your fingers curl around it.

Turn to page 17.

You worm your way through the tall wheat as bullets rocket past you in the night. You grope your way forward, never knowing if you are heading right into another Rebel nest.

Minutes go by. You're still slowly, blindly crawling. You poke your head up, barely clearing the top of the grass. It's silent now; the firing has quit. You can't see anyone on either side.

You can't know that over the next two days, many thousands of men will trample this same grass, and thousands will never leave it alive. On this soft, moon-cast night, it's almost as if there are no soldiers, no armies, no war. Everything seems the way it should be on a peaceful summer night.

But it really isn't, and you duck back down. You crawl and crawl until finally you hear voices ahead. They're low, almost whispering. Listening carefully, you hear a man talking. He doesn't sound like a Southerner.

"Out here somewhere, eh? Where?"

"How should *I* know?" answers a sharp girl's voice. "Somewhere. Just don't shoot!"

It's her! You peel off your shirt and wave it overhead.

"Here!" you say softly. "Don't shoot!"

"We won't," the man says. "Come in."

When you part the grass onto the Union picket post, the first person you see is Lorena.

"We made it!" she tells you.

"Yep." Grinning, you take off the cap that has hidden her face. You throw it into the tall grass.

Turn to page 101.

110

You've got to see about your family, you decide.

"Listen," you tell Lorena, "I'll just go over to our place real quick. I bet they're fine. I'll let them know I'm okay, and then I'll be back."

Lorena folds her skinny arms. "You do what you got to do," she repeats. "I'll do the same."

"No—wait for me, Rena. I'll be back. I'll help you, if I can."

But Rena doesn't answer. She just watches you. As you step quietly up the stairs, you swear to yourself that if you can make it, you'll get back.

You climb and scurry through the rest of the back alleys. Your house also looks deserted. Stepping inside, you hear footsteps—heavy steps, like boots—on the stairs.

"Who's that?" you call. "Father?"

At the top of the stairs a man in gray appears. He holds a pistol in his hand.

"Who are you?" he asks in a threatening voice. His eyes are black, and his face is gaunt.

You want to run, but you stand solid.

"I live here," you say. "Tell me where my family is. Tell me!"

The Confederate lifts his pistol. He starts to point it.

Turn to page 58.

112

You can't believe Lee means it. Almost a mile of wide-open fields lies between the Rebels and Cemetery Ridge. Can a Confederate charge tomorrow possibly succeed?

"The trouble is," Lee tells you, "I don't really know how much of the Federal force is concentrated there. Today we've attacked the southern end of their line." He motions to the right, where smoke still rises from the bloody battlegrounds that will be known always as Devil's Den, Little Round Top, the Wheat Field, and the Peach Orchard. "They've rushed forces there. This evening we will attack at the other end—at the two hills above Cemetery Ridge. By tomorrow I hope the Union lines will be bunched at those ends and weak in the middle. If my plan succeeds, an all-out charge right here in the center can overwhelm the Federals and win the war."

"But General Lee," you say, "how can you be sure the Union force will be weak in the middle?"

Lee turns to you. His brown eyes sparkle with the challenge. "That's where I hope to rely on you," he says.

Turn to page 96.

Sergeant Hill stops a man carrying two long, rolled-up stretchers. He takes one and hands it to you.

"Now keep up!" he yells over the thundering bombardment. And he dashes back to the front of his drum-turned-stretcher corps.

For a moment you run, too. But it's hard to keep up—the stretcher is awkward and heavy. It twists your arms, and as you run it bangs your hip. The men start to pull away.

You could ditch this thing right now in the fields. Hill isn't looking. You'd be long gone before he realized it.

But the battle is starting, and people are going to be hurt—Rebels *and* Yankees. If you join the stretcher-carriers, you could help—and you could see the battle, too.

You've got to choose right now: Billy Bayley's house and possible safety, or the assault on the hill called Little Round Top?

If you run for Billy's house, turn to page 83.

If you join the stretcher corps, turn to page 97.

114

Shaking, suddenly cold, you raise your hands. You turn slowly. Standing there is a slender blond-haired man in a gray coat and hat. He grips a pistol; a sword hangs at his side. He's a Confederate officer.

"Why, you're just a child," he says. "No gun?"

"No, sir."

"Is this place your home?"

"Yes."

He looks at you thoughtfully. "How well do you know the terrain around here?" he asks.

"Why," you say, surprised, "I guess I know it pretty well."

He nods. "Of course you would," he says. "I'd like to take you to General Lee."

"General *Lee?*"

"There's a lot you could tell him," the officer says. "If you help us master this terrain, it'll save a lot of lives in the end. Because one way or another, we're going to win this battle."

You swallow hard as fear creeps up your spine. What's going to happen in Gettysburg?

"But if you run for town right now," the officer says, "I won't shoot. Southern officers don't take young civilians prisoner."

Turn to page 2.

116

"Not much, I don't think," you answer. "He hardly spoke for two minutes."

"But what did he *say?*"

You shrug. "He has a funny, high voice. There were so many people, I couldn't really hear. But everyone says it couldn't have been much of a speech—so short. The other fellow, that Everett, he spoke for nigh on three hours."

You and Lorena start walking back toward town. She glances across Cemetery Ridge, toward the fields where you two escaped to safety—and where, the next two days, thousands of soldiers died.

"I don't guess anyone will remember what those politicians said here," Rena says. "But I hope no one forgets what all those men *did* here."

"You should have made the speech," you tell her. "President Lincoln should have said that."

She laughs, and grows thoughtful. "Did you ever think how there's only Union dead in the cemetery?"

You shrug. "So?"

"All those Confederates, they're just buried out there in the fields, and wherever. It don't seem fair, somehow."

"If they'd won, they'd have the cemetery," you say.

"They'd have a lot more than that," says Lorena.

Go on to the next page.

You ask your friend, "Do you think it was worth it? I mean, for all those young men and even boys to die or be hurt for the rest of their lives, just so we'd have one country and no slaves?"

"Don't know," she answers. "Maybe that's what the president talked about."

"Maybe," you say. "I couldn't really hear."

At first, nobody else takes Lincoln's speech very seriously, either. Even the president thinks it was a failure. It's only gradually that the Gettysburg Address—just 271 words written by a president struggling to put the meaning of this great battle into words—becomes famous as perhaps the most beautiful and meaningful speech in American history.

The End

ABOUT THE AUTHOR

DOUG WILHELM is the author of *Search the Amazon! The Forgotten Planet, Scene of the Crime,* and *The Secret of Mystery Hill* in Bantam's Choose Your Own Adventure series. A freelance writer and editor, Doug lives in Montpelier, Vermont, and has a son, Bradley, who is almost eight years old.

ABOUT THE ILLUSTRATOR

TOM LA PADULA graduated from Parsons School of Design with a B.F.A. and earned his M.F.A. from Syracuse University.

For over a decade Tom has illustrated for national and international magazines, advertising agencies, and publishing houses. Besides his illustrating, Tom is on the faculty of Pratt Institute, where he teaches a class in illustration.

During the spring of 1992, his work was exhibited in the group show "The Art of the Baseball Card" at the Baseball Hall of Fame in Cooperstown, New York. In addition, the corporation Johnson & Johnson recently acquired one of Tom's illustrations for their private collection.

Mr. La Padula has illustrated *Soccer Star, The Secret of Mystery Hill, The Luckiest Day of Your Life,* and *Secret of the Dolphins* in the Choose Your Own Adventure series. He resides in New Rochelle, New York, with his wife, son, and daughter.